THE BIBLE
THE REALLY INTERESTING BITS!

THE BIBLE
THE REALLY INTERESTING BITS!

ILLUSTRATED BY BRIAN DELF

TYNDALE HOUSE PUBLISHERS, INC.
WHEATON, ILLINOIS

A DORLING KINDERSLEY BOOK

Editor Martin Redfern

Art Editor Peter Radcliffe

Project Editor Mary Atkinson

Senior Editor Scarlett O'Hara

Senior Art Editor Vicky Wharton

Senior Managing Editor Linda Martin

Senior Managing Art Editor Julia Harris

DTP Designer Andrew O'Brien

Jacket Designer Joe Hoyle

Production Kate Oliver

US Editors Claudia Volkman, David Barrett

Text by A D Publishing Services Ltd

First published in Great Britain in 1999 by
Dorling Kindersley Limited, London

This edition published in the United States by
Tyndale House Publishers, Inc.
351 Executive Drive
Carol Stream, Illinois 60188

Visit Tyndale's exciting Web site at www.tyndale.com

ISBN 0-8423-3161-1

Colour reproduction by Dot Gradations, Essex
Printed and bound in Spain by AGT

D.L. TO: 1112 - 1999

2 4 6 8 10 9 7 5 3 1

CONTENTS

16.99

Introduction

THE BIBLE CONTAINS some of the most exciting stories ever written. Divided into two parts, the Old and New Testaments, it covers the periods before and after the birth of Jesus 2,000 years ago. Here we bring to life some of the best-known Bible stories in a series of visually stunning panoramas.

The Old Testament begins with the story of Creation. Over a period of six days, God created the heavens and the earth, and filled them with living creatures. On the seventh day, he rested. He was pleased with what he had made and gave Adam and Eve the Garden of Eden to care for, but they sinned against God and were driven out of Eden in disgrace.

Only Noah continued to follow God's ways. God decided to start again; he told Noah to build an ark, in which he was to put his family and two of every living creature. Then God flooded the earth. Afterwards, God promised he would never again destroy the world by a flood.

Many years later, God chose Abraham, a man of faith, to be the father of a great nation. God promised that he would give this nation a land to live in – the land of Canaan. Abraham and his descendents grew into the twelve tribes of Israel. Many of the stories in the Old Testament are about the Israelites gaining, and then keeping, the Promised Land.

From Canaan, the Israelites went to live in Egypt, where they became slaves. God chose Moses, an Israelite brought up by an Egyptian princess, to lead them out of Egypt back to the Promised Land. The story of the Exodus tells of the Israelites' escape across the Red Sea and Moses receiving the Ten Commandments.

When the Israelites finally entered Canaan, the land was ruled by judges, such as Samson, and then kings, such as David and Solomon. But after a time, people turned from God and started to worship idols. Israel was invaded and conquered, the temple was destroyed, and God's people were exiled in far-off Babylon. Eventually, they were allowed to return, and the temple was rebuilt.

Hundreds of years passed, but God's people never forgot the prophets' promise of a Savior. At the beginning of the New Testament, Israel was part of the Roman Empire and the people were hoping for a leader who would free them from Roman rule. When the Savior, Jesus Christ, was born in Bethlehem in Judea 2,000 years ago, he was visited by humble shepherds and wise men from a distant land, who came to worship the new king.

At the age of thirty, Jesus chose twelve disciples and began to live the life of a traveling teacher and healer. Crowds of people flocked from far and wide to see him cure the sick and perform other amazing miracles.

Jesus used everyday stories or parables to illustrate his teachings and to make them more understandable to his listeners. Some of Jesus' most memorable teaching is contained in the Sermon on the Mount. Jesus intended this as a guide for his disciples to show them how to live as members of the kingdom of God.

However, the religious authorities were suspicious of Jesus. After entering Jerusalem to celebrate the Passover, he was arrested, tried, and sentenced to death by the Roman governor Pontius Pilate. In agony, Jesus died on the cross. His body was laid in a rock tomb, and a heavy stone was rolled across the entrance to seal it.

Three days later, the stone had been rolled away – Jesus had risen from the dead! He appeared to his followers on several occasions before returning to heaven. He told his disciples to pass on the Good News of his life, death, and resurrection to the whole world, and he promised to send them the Holy Spirit to help them in their task.

Despite opposition and persecution, more and more people believed the disciples' message; they became known as Christians. On his three missionary journeys, Paul took the message of Jesus to other parts of the Roman Empire. The book ends with Paul in Rome, writing the letters that have inspired millions of Christians over the last 2,000 years to become followers of Jesus Christ.

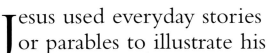

In the Beginning

Some people believe that the fruit eaten by Adam and Eve in the Garden of Eden was a pomegranate.

IN THE VERY BEGINNING, even before the existence of time, there was nothing but God. He was everywhere, and he was always present.

When God began creating the heavens and the earth, the earth was without shape or order. It was a dark, empty mass. But God saw that it was full of enormous potential.

God's powerful Spirit moved over the shapeless earth. He knew that he could create something wonderful out of nothing. He knew that he could create color and beauty, texture and shape, stillness and movement. He knew that he could make things that were strong and hard, and other things that were soft and delicate. He imagined things that would be good to look at, and he thought of a million different sounds, tastes, and smells.

And so God set to work, to make and to order. Over a period of six days, he created the heavens and the earth and filled them with living things. On the seventh day, he rested. Every part of his creation was special, unique, and perfect. Everything that he made was good.

From the beginning, God has always shown that he is a powerful Creator, one who loves and cares for all the wonderful things that he has made.

THE FIRST DAY
Suddenly God spoke. "Let there be light!" he said. As soon as he had uttered these words, the very first light shone. God took the light, and he separated it from the darkness. He called the light "day" and the darkness "night." As the dusk fell and the dawn came, God saw that it was good.

THE FOURTH DAY
Then God made time, with seasons, days, and years. He made the fiery sun to shine throughout the day, bringing heat and light to the earth. He made the silvery moon to shine throughout the coolness of the night. Then God studded the night sky with stars and planets. He knew that his creation was good.

GOD CREATES ADAM
When God made man, he formed him from the dust of the earth. God breathed life into him, and he became Adam, a living being. But Adam was lonely. He wanted a companion.

GOD CREATES EVE
"It isn't good for you to be alone," said God. But there was no one else like Adam. Therefore while Adam was in a deep sleep, God removed one of his ribs. From it, God made Eve, the first woman.

THE GARDEN OF EDEN
God gave Adam and Eve the Garden of Eden to care for, and he brought them all the animals that he had created so that they could name them. In this way, God showed his love for humanity.

THE SECOND DAY

God looked at the waters and mists swirling around the earth, catching the light that he had created. "I will separate the waters," God said, "and I will make sky." God divided the waters and mists, and circled the waters with sky. Evening came; it was the end of the second day.

THE THIRD DAY

"I will create the seas and the dry ground," said God. Land appeared, but it was empty. "Let plants, trees, seeds, and fruit fill the earth!" God said. Green shoots began to spring up and cover the ground. They dug their roots deep into the earth, and leaves began to grow. God was pleased with what he saw.

THE FIFTH DAY

"Let the seas and the sky be filled with life!" said God. Immediately fish of every kind shimmered in the blue-green waters of the sea. Butterflies, birds, bats, and bees hummed, hovered, swooped, and soared across the sky. God was pleased. He knew that everything he had made was good.

THE SIXTH AND SEVENTH DAYS

"Now I will fill the earth!" said God. Every kind of creature, wild and tame, leaped, slithered, and crawled across the land. "I will make people," God said. "They will be like me: they will be masters over all life." When he had finished his creation, God rested.

Cherubim and a flaming sword stood guard over the Garden of Eden.

FORBIDDEN FRUIT

"Enjoy everything in the garden," God told Adam and Eve, "but do not eat from the tree of the knowledge of good and evil, or you will die." But Satan disguised himself as a snake. "Don't listen!" he whispered to Eve. "Eat and you will be like God." Adam and Eve ate. Suddenly, they felt guilty and were afraid.

DRIVEN OUT OF EDEN

Adam and Eve tried to hide, but God knew that they had disobeyed him. "As a punishment, you will have to leave the Garden of Eden," God said sadly. "You will be unhappy and will feel pain. Your lives will be difficult, and eventually you will die." But God never stopped loving them.

Noah and the Flood

ADAM AND EVE HAD TWO SONS called Cain and Abel. Cain was jealous because God preferred Abel's generous offerings and one day, in a fit of anger, Cain killed his brother. God was greatly saddened by this. Years passed, and few people remembered God at all. They argued and fought; they were selfish and greedy. God was sorry that he had ever made people, and he decided to start again. Only one person, a man called Noah, was different from the rest. He was a good man, and he knew God.

NOAH BUILDS THE ARK

God told Noah his plan. "I am going to destroy everything I have made with a flood," he said, "but I will save you. You must build an ark, which will keep you and your family safe from the flood." Then God told Noah exactly how to build the ark.

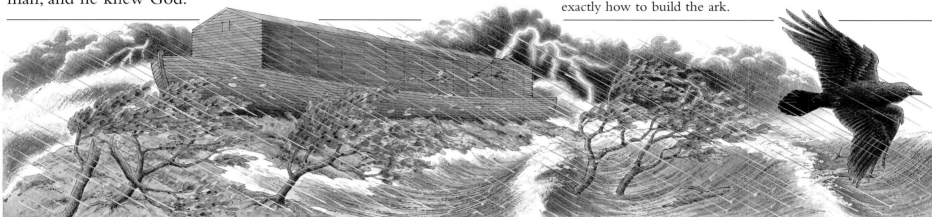

THE GREAT FLOOD

Then it began to rain. It rained and rained for forty days and forty nights. The rivers rose and burst their banks. The waters grew deeper and deeper until all the towns and villages, mountains, and forests were covered by the flood waters. Everything was destroyed. Only Noah, his family, and the animals were safe in the ark, with God watching over them. At last, the rain stopped, and a strong wind blew. Slowly, the waters began to go down. One day, Noah opened a window and sent out a raven to see if the land was dry. The raven flew back and forth, but it was unable to find any dry ground, so Noah knew that the earth was still covered with flood water.

The ark came to rest on Mount Ararat, in modern-day Turkey.

A rainbow appeared as a sign that God would never again destroy the earth by a flood.

All the animals left the ark, one after another.

LEAVING THE ARK

"Now it is safe for you to leave the ark," said God. "Take your family and all the animals with you. The earth is yours to enjoy!" Noah and his family walked out of the ark and onto the dry land. The animals leaped and bounded across the ground, free at last. Noah's first task was to build an altar. He wanted to thank God for keeping his family and all the animals safe during the flood. "I promise that I will never again destroy the earth by flood," said God. "And as long as the earth remains, there will always be times to plant and times to harvest, heat and cold, days and years. Look at the rainbow in the sky. It is a sign that I will keep my promise to you for ever," he said.

The animals went into the ark, two by two.

THE ANIMALS ENTER THE ARK

When the ark was finished, God said, "I want you to take the male and female of every kind of living creature into the ark. Make sure that you have plenty of food for the animals and to feed yourselves. Soon it will start to rain, and the flood will begin. Then everything I have made will be destroyed. I will keep you and your family safe because I know that you love me." Noah prepared the ark, and when it was ready, the animals came to him. They trotted and cantered, slithered and scuttled, scampered and flew to Noah and the safety of the ark. Then Noah and his wife, his three sons, and their wives went inside, and God shut the door.

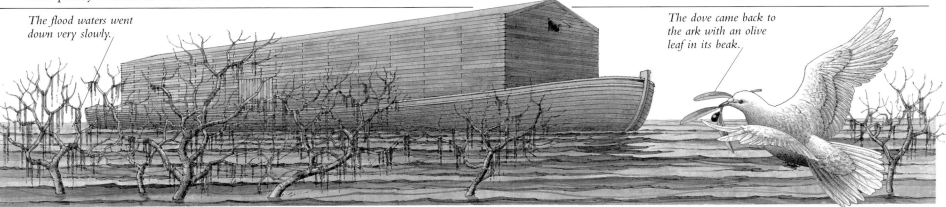

The flood waters went down very slowly.

The dove came back to the ark with an olive leaf in its beak.

NOAH SENDS OUT A DOVE

Noah waited. The days passed, each one very much like the last. Then Noah took one of the doves and set it free. He watched as the dove stretched its wings and flew away. But again the bird soon returned, and Noah knew that the waters still covered the earth. Seven days later, Noah freed the dove again and waited. That evening, the dove returned with an olive leaf in its beak. The waters were almost gone. Noah waited another week before releasing the dove once more. But this time the dove did not come back. Noah guessed correctly that it had found somewhere to rest. The flood waters had finally gone, and the land was dry.

The tower reached high up into the sky.

Mud bricks, dried in the sun, were used to build the tower.

THE TOWER OF BABEL

But many years later, the people forgot God once more. They discovered that they could do many clever things and became full of their own importance. They settled on the plains of Babylonia, and one day, they had a brilliant idea. "Let's build a tower that reaches up to heaven," they said. "Then everyone will know how important we are!" Everybody was talking about it, for they all spoke the same language. God saw how proud they were. "I must stop them," he said. So God made them speak different languages, and they could no longer understand each other. After that, the people abandoned the tower and settled in different places, each speaking their own language.

The Family of Abraham

Abraham answered God's call and set out with his people for the land of Canaan.

MANY YEARS after Noah, God chose a man called Abraham to follow him. God promised Abraham that he would have a son, and that his descendants would become a great nation with a land of their own. God kept his promise. In his old age, Abraham had a son called Isaac, and his descendants became God's "chosen people."

ABRAHAM'S JOURNEY

Abraham's father had taken his family from the city of Ur to Haran. One day, God spoke to Abraham: "I want you to leave Haran and go to a new land, which I will give to you and your descendants."

GOD'S PROMISE OF A SON

Abraham and his wife, Sarah, went from place to place, living in tents. When they reached Canaan, God promised Abraham, "You will have a son, and your descendants will be as numerous as the stars."

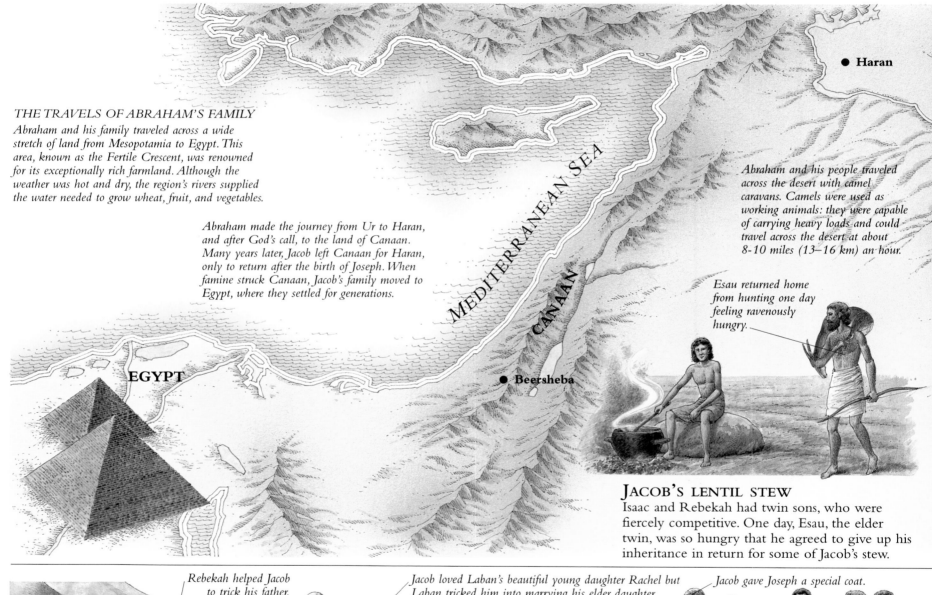

THE TRAVELS OF ABRAHAM'S FAMILY
Abraham and his family traveled across a wide stretch of land from Mesopotamia to Egypt. This area, known as the Fertile Crescent, was renowned for its exceptionally rich farmland. Although the weather was hot and dry, the region's rivers supplied the water needed to grow wheat, fruit, and vegetables.

Abraham made the journey from Ur to Haran, and after God's call, to the land of Canaan. Many years later, Jacob left Canaan for Haran, only to return after the birth of Joseph. When famine struck Canaan, Jacob's family moved to Egypt, where they settled for generations.

● **Haran**

MEDITERRANEAN SEA

CANAAN

EGYPT

● **Beersheba**

Abraham and his people traveled across the desert with camel caravans. Camels were used as working animals: they were capable of carrying heavy loads and could travel across the desert at about 8-10 miles (13–16 km) an hour.

Esau returned home from hunting one day feeling ravenously hungry.

JACOB'S LENTIL STEW

Isaac and Rebekah had twin sons, who were fiercely competitive. One day, Esau, the elder twin, was so hungry that he agreed to give up his inheritance in return for some of Jacob's stew.

Rebekah helped Jacob to trick his father.

Jacob loved Laban's beautiful young daughter Rachel but Laban tricked him into marrying his elder daughter Leah. Jacob was finally allowed to marry Rachel in return for working a further seven years without pay.

Jacob gave Joseph a special coat.

THE STOLEN BLESSING

Isaac wanted to bless Esau, his elder son, but Jacob disguised himself as his hairy brother, and tricked his dying father into giving him the blessing. "He's stolen what was mine!" cried Esau. "I will kill him!"

JACOB MARRIES LEAH AND RACHEL

Jacob ran for his life! But God promised to bless him. Jacob went to work for his uncle Laban and married Leah and Rachel. When he returned to Canaan with his family, he made peace with Esau.

THE FAVORITE SON

Jacob had twelve sons, but he loved Joseph the most and gave him a beautiful multicolored coat. Joseph had strange dreams that seemed to predict the future. His brothers were jealous of him.

THE THREE VISITORS

Many years later, Abraham still had no son. Then three messengers from God arrived. "In a year's time, Sarah will have a son," they said. Sarah heard this. "I'm too old to have a baby!" she laughed.

THE GIFT OF LAUGHTER

When Abraham was 100 years old, God kept his promise and Sarah had a son. She called him Isaac, meaning laughter. "God has given me laughter in my old age!" she said. Abraham loved Isaac greatly.

A WIFE FOR ISAAC

When Isaac was older, Abraham sent his servant back to Haran to choose a wife for Isaac. "Show me the right person," the servant prayed to God. When he saw Rebekah, he knew she was God's choice.

Rebekah was drawing water from a well when Abraham's servant saw her.

The remains of a ziggurat have been found in Ur. These pyramid-like buildings had outside staircases leading to a temple at the top.

MESOPOTAMIA

Tigris River

Euphrates River

Tents provided ideal temporary homes for the desert wanderers. They would often set them up on the outskirts of large towns.

Ur ●

Abraham and his family led a nomadic life. They traveled from place to place, looking for grazing land and water for their animals. They followed the many trade routes that had been established by that time.

Ur, in modern-day Iraq, was one of the most important cities in Mesopotamia.

Joseph's coat was dipped in goat's blood.

Joseph correctly interpreted Pharaoh's strange dreams.

Joseph was now an important Egyptian official.

JOSEPH IS SOLD AS A SLAVE

"Let's get rid of Joseph!" his brothers plotted. They sold him as a slave to some passing traders, who were traveling to Egypt. "Joseph has been killed by a wild animal," the brothers lied to their father.

PHARAOH'S DREAMS

God looked after Joseph by helping him to explain Pharaoh's dreams. When Joseph predicted a terrible famine, Pharaoh put him in charge of storing food, and there was plenty to eat for all.

GOD'S PEOPLE SETTLE IN EGYPT

Joseph's brothers left Canaan for Egypt in search of food. Joseph forgave them for what they had done to him. He sent for his father and was overjoyed to see him. The whole family settled in Egypt.

The Exodus

JOSEPH'S WISDOM HAD SAVED Egypt from a terrible fate during the famine, and from that time on Joseph's family made the land of the Pharaohs their home. Over many generations they grew into the twelve tribes of Israel. For hundreds of years, the Israelites lived peacefully alongside the Egyptians. Many became wealthy and rose to positions of great influence in Egyptian society. But as time passed, the Egyptians began to feel threatened by the increasing number of Israelites, and they forgot what Joseph had done for them all those years ago.

THE ISRAELITES IN SLAVERY

"There are too many Israelites in Egypt," complained the new pharaoh. "We must make them our slaves, or they will plot against us." So the Israelites were forced to work in the fields and to build cities for the Egyptians. They were often whipped and beaten. But their numbers continued to grow.

After each plague, Pharaoh stubbornly refused to let the Israelites go. The Egyptians began to despair as the plagues destroyed their animals and crops.

THE TEN PLAGUES

"God says that you must free the Israelites," Moses told Pharaoh. But Pharaoh did not listen. "Terrible things will happen if you disobey God," warned Moses. Pharaoh ignored him and, the next day, the Nile River turned to blood. Soon afterwards, all of Egypt was covered with frogs. But still Pharaoh refused to give in. More plagues followed: the air filled with clouds of gnats, then swarms of flies; cows and sheep died in the fields; people and animals were covered in boils; hail beat down; and locusts ate the crops. Then darkness covered Egypt. God told Moses, "Every firstborn child and animal in Egypt will die tonight and Pharaoh will beg you to leave."

Manna was white and tasted of honey.

Moses struck a rock and water gushed out for the thirsty Israelites to drink.

FOOD IN THE DESERT

Moses led the Israelites into the desert where there was no food. "We were better off in Egypt!" the people complained. "I will give you food," said God. That evening, there was quail to eat and in the morning, white flakes covered the ground. "It is manna from God," Moses told the people. "It is good to eat."

THE TEN COMMANDMENTS

"God wants to speak to us," said Moses. "Prepare yourselves." A thick cloud came down, and Moses climbed God's holy mountain. There God gave Moses two large stones with the Ten Commandments written on them. "You are my people. These are my laws," said God. "Keep them, and you will be blessed."

The Egyptian princess took the baby to live in the pharaoh's palace.

Moses was tending his flock on the far side of the desert when he came upon the burning bush.

HIDDEN IN A BASKET
When Pharaoh ordered the killing of all Israelite baby boys, Jochebed, an Israelite, hid her son Moses in a basket by the River Nile. Pharaoh's daughter found the baby and looked after him.

MOSES KILLS AN EGYPTIAN
As Moses grew older, he saw how the Israelites suffered. Once, he witnessed an Egyptian beating an Israelite slave. In his anger, Moses killed the Egyptian. Somebody saw him and he had to hide.

MOSES AND THE BURNING BUSH
Moses left Egypt and became a shepherd. One day, he saw a bush that was on fire but did not burn up. From the bush, God's voice said, "Moses, you will lead the Israelites out of Egypt."

When the Egyptian army chased the Israelites across the Red Sea, the waters crashed over them, and they were drowned.

Moses led the Israelites to safety.

THE ISRAELITES ESCAPE
The Israelites ate a special meal and made plans to leave. God told them what to do to save themselves: they were to mark their doors with lambs' blood, so that death would "pass over" their homes. That night, the firstborn son of every Egyptian family died. "Go!" Pharaoh shouted at Moses. The Israelites reached the Red Sea with Pharaoh's army following them. Then Moses said, "Don't be afraid!" and he held out his staff. A strong wind blew and the waters divided, revealing a path to the other side. The Egyptians saw the Israelites walk safely across, and they galloped after them. "Stretch out your hand again," said God. Moses did so, and the waters fell back, drowning the Egyptians.

The people danced and feasted in front of the calf.   *The high priest*

THE GOLDEN CALF
At the foot of the mountain, the people wondered what had happened to Moses. They grew impatient. "Let's make our own god!" they said. So they made a golden calf and worshipped it. When Moses returned, he saw the golden calf and was furious. "You must worship only God," he cried.

BUILDING THE TABERNACLE
"God wants us to erect a special tent where we can worship him," Moses told the people. The finished tent, called the tabernacle, held the ark of the covenant, a chest containing the Ten Commandments. The tabernacle became the focus of religious life; it was erected wherever the Israelites set up camp.

Israel and the Promised Land

Four priests carried the ark of the covenant.

The Jordan River dried up.

MOSES LED GOD'S PEOPLE from Egypt to the edge of Canaan, the Promised Land. He sent spies ahead into this new land to see whether the tribes who lived there were hostile. Although Joshua and Caleb came back with a good report about Canaan, others told frightening stories of giants and fortified cities. The Israelites were scared and refused to go on. As a result, God made them wander in the desert for 40 years. When Moses died, God chose Joshua to be the leader of the Israelites.

CROSSING THE JORDAN RIVER

"Get ready to enter the land I have promised you," God told Joshua. Everyone prepared themselves. First, the priests stepped into the Jordan River carrying the ark of the covenant, which contained God's law. Immediately, the water stopped flowing, and the Israelites walked across dry land into Canaan.

Samson's hair, the key to his strength, was cut while he slept.

SAMSON AND DELILAH

The Israelites had many leaders who led them into battle. Among them was Samson, whom God had given superhuman strength. When Samson fell in love with the Philistine woman Delilah, she made him tell her the secret of his strength – his hair. When his hair was cut off, his strength disappeared.

SAMSON DESTROYS THE TEMPLE

The Philistines took Samson prisoner and tortured him. Then they brought him to their temple to mock him. But Samson prayed to God. "Remember me," he pleaded, "and return my strength." Then Samson pushed against the pillars; they crumbled and fell, crushing Samson and everyone in the temple.

David refused to wear armor when he fought Goliath.

DAVID AND GOLIATH

The Philistines had a champion called Goliath. He was huge – over nine feet tall – and he did not follow Israel's God. Twice a day Goliath stood in front of the Israelite army and shouted, "Who will fight me?" Nobody dared! Then one day David went to the Israelite camp. When he heard Goliath's challenge, he said, "Why should we be afraid? God is on our side. I will fight Goliath." David took his sling and five smooth stones. Goliath sneered when he saw David. But David swung his sling around in the air at high speed. A stone struck Goliath on the forehead, and he fell down dead. Then David took Goliath's own sword and cut off Goliath's head.

The real mother would rather give her child away than see him cut in half.

King Solomon demonstrated his famous wisdom.

SOLOMON'S WISDOM

David's son Solomon was famous for his great wisdom, a gift from God. One day, two women were arguing over who was the mother of a baby. Solomon ordered, "Cut the baby in half!" When one woman pleaded, "Give the other woman the baby. Don't kill him!" Solomon knew she was the real mother.

KING SOLOMON'S TEMPLE

In Jerusalem, King Solomon built a beautiful temple, where people could worship God. The temple contained bronze pillars and golden furniture; its stone walls were lined with cedar wood and covered with gold. The ark of the covenant was kept in the holiest part of the temple.

The city walls began to crumble.

THE FALL OF JERICHO

Now the fortified city of Jericho lay ahead, its huge gates shut against them. Joshua obeyed God's instructions. For six days the Israelite army marched around the city walls, while seven priests with ram's horns marched in front of the ark of the covenant. On the seventh day, they marched seven times. When the priests blew their horns, Joshua ordered, "Shout! God has given us the city of Jericho!" The walls began to crumble and Jericho was theirs. Only Rahab and her family were kept safe because she had hidden the spies Joshua had sent into the city. The Israelites made their home in Canaan and, when they were obedient to God, they prospered there.

On one occasion, Saul flew into a furious rage and threw his spear at David.

GOD SPEAKS TO SAMUEL

Time passed, and people forgot to follow God's ways. But God spoke to a boy called Samuel, at the temple in Shiloh. Three times God called his name. The last time, Samuel realized it was God.

SAUL IS MADE KING

Samuel grew up to be a priest, through whom God spoke to the Israelites. When they asked for a king, Samuel said, "God is our king!" But God said, "Grant them their wish. Anoint Saul king of Israel."

SAUL AND DAVID

At first, King Saul obeyed God. But he became disobedient. When he was moody, a shepherd boy called David played music to calm him down. In secret, God chose David to be Israel's future king.

David danced at the head of the procession.

THE ARK ENTERS JERUSALEM

When Saul died, the Israelites wanted David to be their king. "God has chosen you to lead us!" they cried. So David became king, and he defeated Israel's enemies. He wanted to give thanks to God. "Bring the ark of the covenant to Jerusalem, where it will stay," ordered David, "and tell everyone to come and celebrate." So, as Levite priests carried the ark into Jerusalem, musicians played, choirs sang songs of praise, and everyone shouted with joy. David danced in front of the ark, praising God. His wife, Michal, watched scornfully. She thought David looked foolish. But God said to David, "I will make you great, and I will bless your descendants."

The Queen's servants carried gifts for Solomon.

The Queen of Sheba

King Solomon

THE VISIT OF THE QUEEN OF SHEBA

Far away, the Queen of Sheba heard tales of King Solomon's wisdom and wealth. She wanted to know if they were true, and traveled more than 1,200 miles with her officials and servants to visit the king. She brought gifts of gold, spices, and precious jewels. She talked to Solomon, who answered all her questions. "I was told stories of your greatness," she said, "but your wisdom and riches are even greater than I imagined. Your people must be so happy to be ruled by you. I want to praise your God for all that he has given you and for the love that he has shown to his people." Then she and Solomon exchanged gifts and she returned to her home country.

A People in Exile

THE DEATH OF KING SOLOMON was followed by arguments and civil wars, and the land that God had given his people was divided into two: Israel and Judah. Many of God's people turned away from him to worship idols. For more than 200 years, God sent prophets to warn his people that they would be punished for their sinful ways. Because they did not listen, they paid the price. First the Assyrians came, then the Babylonians. Israel was conquered and Judah was invaded. Many people were exiled to the far-off land of Babylon.

Meshach   Daniel   Shadrach   Babylonian official   Abednego

EXILES IN BABYLON

"Find me the finest young men from Judah," ordered King Nebuchadnezzar of Babylon. "Teach them Babylonian. Train them for three years, and then they will work for me." Shadrach, Meshach, Abednego, and Daniel were chosen. All four continued to worship God, even though they lived in a foreign land.

The city walls were knocked down.

The temple and other buildings were in flames.

THE FALL OF JERUSALEM

Back in Jerusalem, Nebuchadnezzar left Zedekiah, king of Judah, in charge of the remaining Jews. But when Zedekiah tried to trick Nebuchadnezzar, the Babylonians besieged the city. God sent the prophet Jeremiah to warn his people: "If you surrender, God will save you." But they did not follow his advice. The Babylonian army then stormed the walls and ran into Jerusalem, stealing all the bronze, silver, and gold from the temple, before destroying the city by fire. Zedekiah was captured and his sons were executed. Then he was blinded, put in shackles, and led away to Babylon with the rest of God's people. Jeremiah was allowed to stay behind with the few poor people who were left.

Ezekiel   Dry bones represented the scattered exiles.   Flesh grew on the skeletons and they came to life.   Jeshua   Zerubbabel   The foundations of the temple   Cedar logs from Lebanon

A VISION OF HOPE

In a vision, the prophet Ezekiel saw a valley of dry bones, representing the captive Jews, scattered and dead. "Speak my words to these bones so they may live," said God. As Ezekiel spoke, the bones formed skeletons and grew flesh, a promise that the scattered exiles would one day be reunited and free.

REBUILDING THE TEMPLE

When Cyrus of Persia ruled Babylon, he decreed, "God's people may return to Jerusalem to rebuild the temple." He gave them money and supplies, and silver and gold, which had been stolen from the temple years before. Zerubbabel and Jeshua returned and started the rebuilding work. It took many years to finish.

NEBUCHADNEZZAR'S GOLD STATUE

Musicians began to play as a signal to bow down before the statue.

Babylon was full of statues representing different gods. Nebuchadnezzar set a huge gold statue on the Dura plain. "Everyone must worship it," he ordered. "Anyone who disobeys will be thrown into a fiery furnace." At the signal, everyone fell to their knees, except Shadrach, Meshach, and Abednego.

THE FIERY FURNACE

The young exiles were tied up and thrown into the red-hot furnace. Suddenly Nebuchadnezzar cried out, "Four men are walking in the fire! And one looks like an angel!" Shadrach, Meshach, and Abednego stepped out of the furnace unharmed. "Your God has rescued you. How great he is!" cried the king.

Daniel was seen praying to God, and Darius was forced to arrest him.

King Darius was relieved to see that Daniel had not been killed by the lions.

THE PLOT AGAINST DANIEL

Years later in Babylon, Darius the Mede came to the throne and made Daniel a top official. Daniel's enemies persuaded Darius to make a law forbidding anyone to pray, unless it was to the king; anyone who broke the law would be thrown into the lions' den. But Daniel continued to pray faithfully to God.

DANIEL IS THROWN TO THE LIONS

Darius knew he had been tricked, but he could do nothing. "May your God rescue you," he said as the entrance to the den was sealed behind Daniel. That night, Darius could not sleep. At dawn he rushed to the lions' den. "Daniel?" he called. "I am safe!" Daniel replied. "God's angel has shut the lions' mouths."

Masons carved stone blocks.

Workers labored from sunrise to sunset.

Ezra read out God's law in front of the rebuilt temple.

The people wept as they confessed their sins.

NEHEMIAH REBUILDS THE CITY WALLS

In far-off Susa, King Artaxerxes' cupbearer, Nehemiah, heard that the walls of Jerusalem were still broken down, and this saddened him greatly. He prayed for God's help, and gained the king's permission to go to Jerusalem. Despite enemy attacks, Nehemiah's team completed the rebuilding in 52 days.

THE PROMISE OF A NEW KING

When Jerusalem was rebuilt, Ezra the priest read God's laws to the people. They began weeping as they realized how disobedient they had been. They repented and worshipped God. Through his prophets, God promised to send a new king, the Messiah, who would save the people and reveal God's love to them.

Jesus' Birth and Early Life

FOR HUNDREDS OF YEARS, God's people were ruled by different foreign powers until eventually they became part of the Roman Empire. Some people remembered the prophets' message: that God would send his Savior into the world. They hoped for a soldier-king who would deliver them from the Romans. But when God's Savior, Jesus, was born around 2,000 years ago, he came with a message of peace. He spoke of God's love for all people, of the forgiveness of sins, and of a new way of life for his followers.

The angel Gabriel told Mary not to be afraid.

THE ANGEL'S MESSAGE

One day, the angel Gabriel came to Mary, who was engaged to be married to a carpenter called Joseph. "Don't be afraid!" said the angel. "God has chosen you to be the mother of his Son. Call the baby Jesus, which means 'savior.'" Mary was amazed but she said, "I will do whatever God wants."

The heavens rang out with the sound of angels praising God.

The shepherds left their fields to worship the baby Jesus.

THE SHEPHERDS' CALL

That night, shepherds were looking after their sheep on the hills when suddenly an angel appeared. The shepherds were terrified, but the angel said, "I bring good news. God's Savior has been born tonight. You will find the baby lying in a manger." Then the sky filled with angels saying, "Glory to God!"

THE BABY IN THE MANGER

Mary's baby was born that night in the stable. Mary and Joseph named him Jesus. There was no cradle for him, so they wrapped him in strips of cloth and he slept in a manger. Soon the shepherds arrived to see the baby and discovered that what the angel had told them was true!

VISIT TO THE TEMPLE

When Jesus was twelve, his parents took him to Jerusalem. On the way home, they realized he was missing. They found him in the temple, talking to teachers, who were amazed by his knowledge.

JOHN BAPTIZES JESUS

John baptized people in the Jordan River as a sign that they had turned away from their sins. He was surprised when Jesus came to be baptized, as he had done no wrong. But God said, "This is my Son!"

TEMPTED BY THE DEVIL

God's enemy, Satan, came to test Jesus, to see if he would disobey God and use the power God had given him selfishly. Three times the devil tempted Jesus; three times Jesus resisted.

Mary was obviously pregnant.

MARY VISITS ELIZABETH

The angel told Mary that her cousin Elizabeth was also expecting a baby, so Mary went to visit her. Before Mary spoke, Elizabeth knew her news. "God has blessed you in a special way!" she cried.

THE ROAD TO BETHLEHEM

Some time later, the Roman governor Caesar Augustus ordered a census. Everyone had to go to their family town to be counted, so Mary traveled with Joseph to Bethlehem. It was a long journey along dusty roads. Mary was due to have her baby very soon, but Bethlehem was so overcrowded with visitors that all the inns in the town were already full. It was late, and the only place Mary and Joseph could find to stay was in a stable.

A star appeared above the stable where Jesus was born.

The wise men traveled on camels from their home in the east. They carried with them gifts of gold, frankincense, and myrrh.

The shepherds told Mary and Joseph about the angel's message, and how a choir of angels had sung praises to God. Then they returned to the fields, thanking God for all the wonderful things they had heard and seen. Mary thought about the shepherds' story, and how she had been chosen to be the mother of God's Savior. She knew this was a very special baby.

THE JOURNEY OF THE WISE MEN

Far away in another country, some wise men saw a new star, a sign that a king had been born. They left their land and followed the star until they found Jesus in a house in Bethlehem. There they worshipped the baby king and presented him with gifts of gold, frankincense, and myrrh.

THE FIRST DISCIPLES

One day, as Jesus walked by the Sea of Galilee, he saw Peter and Andrew fishing. "Follow me," said Jesus, "and you will catch people for God." Immediately, they left their fishing nets to follow Jesus. They were joined by two other fishermen, James and John. These four men became Jesus' first followers.

JESUS' FIRST MIRACLE AT CANA

Mary, Jesus' mother, was invited to a wedding in Cana with Jesus and his disciples. During the party, the wine ran out and Mary turned to Jesus for help. Jesus said to the servants, "Fill those big pots with water." When the servants poured from the pots, the water had changed into the finest wine.

Jesus' Ministry

WHEN JESUS WAS THIRTY YEARS OLD, he began to attract large crowds who came to hear him preach about God, and to see him heal the sick. But Jesus was not just a teacher or a miracle-worker. He talked about God in a new way, teaching that God's love and forgiveness was for everyone. Jesus treated all people equally and the way he lived was a perfect example of the message he taught. Jesus began his public ministry in Galilee, the northernmost province of Palestine, and it was here, near the town of Capernaum, that he performed many of his miracles.

Jesus explained his special message.

THE WOMAN AT THE WELL

Jesus asked a Samaritan woman to give him some water from a well. She was surprised, as Jews despised Samaritans. But Jesus said, "If you knew who I was, you would ask *me* for some water. People who drink this water will soon be thirsty again, but those who drink my living water will never thirst."

Thousands of people followed Jesus into the quiet desert region near Bethsaida.

The crowd had been listening to Jesus all day and, as evening approached, there was nowhere for them to buy food.

A young boy came forward with his picnic of five bread rolls and two fishes.

GALILEE

Cana ●

Nazareth ●

SAMARIA

FEEDING THE FIVE THOUSAND

Everywhere Jesus went crowds of people followed him. When Jesus had finished teaching early one evening, he told the disciples to feed the crowd. "But there are over five thousand people here!" they cried. Then Andrew said, "This boy has five barley rolls and two fishes." Jesus took the bread and fishes, thanked God for them, and passed them around. Not only did everyone have plenty to eat but the disciples picked up twelve baskets of leftovers!

JUDEA

Emmaus ●

Jerusalem ●

LAZARUS RAISED FROM THE DEAD

Mary and Martha sent for Jesus because their brother Lazarus was ill. But before Jesus arrived, Lazarus died. "If you had come sooner, he would still be alive!" Martha cried. "Have faith!" Jesus said. Then he went to the tomb and ordered the stone to be moved. "Come out!" he called, and Lazarus emerged – alive!

The Sea of Galilee was often stormy.

JESUS HEALS A PARALYZED MAN

A paralyzed man was carried by four friends to the house where Jesus was preaching. The house was so crowded that they had to lower the man on a mat through a hole in the roof. When Jesus saw their faith, he said to the man, "Your sins are forgiven." To everyone's surprise, the man stood up and walked.

JESUS CALMS A STORM

Jesus and his disciples were on a boat one evening when suddenly a violent storm blew up. Jesus had fallen asleep, so the disciples woke him. "Help us!" they cried, "We're going to drown!" Jesus ordered the wind and the waves to be still and, to the amazement of the disciples, there was complete calm.

LAKE HULEH

Capernaum
Bethsaida

SEA OF GALILEE

Tiberias

Gadara

Jordan River

Jericho

DEAD SEA

Many of the events of Jesus' ministry took place on the shores and in the towns around the Sea of Galilee. Fishing was Galilee's main industry and this freshwater lake provided a rich source of fish.

Jesus' appearance changed and his clothing became dazzling white.

Elijah

Moses

The disciples hid their faces in fear.

THE TRANSFIGURATION

Jesus led Peter, James, and John up a mountain to pray. Suddenly Jesus' face began to shine like the sun and his clothing glowed a brilliant white. Then two men appeared, whom Peter recognized as Moses and Elijah. At that moment a bright cloud covered the three men and a voice said, "This is my Son. Listen to him." The disciples fell to the ground in fear. "Do not be afraid," Jesus said, "and tell no one about this until I have come back from the dead."

Jesus angered the crowd by associating with a sinner.

Zacchaeus climbed a sycamore tree to see.

JESUS MEETS ZACCHAEUS

In Jericho, large crowds of people came to see Jesus. Zacchaeus, a wealthy tax collector, was so short that he had to climb a tree to get a glimpse of Jesus. Jesus called out, "Come down, Zacchaeus, and take me to your home." Zacchaeus was amazed – nobody liked tax collectors! But after talking to Jesus, he promised to change his ways. "I will give half my money to the poor, and I will repay four times the amount I have cheated," Zacchaeus said.

Jesus' Teaching

JESUS OFTEN USED STORIES when he was teaching about God. These stories, or parables, were very effective because they referred to ordinary, everyday things that people could understand. He used them to explain to people that God loved them and to demonstrate to his followers how they should live their lives. Sometimes his stories had hidden meanings, and Jesus later explained these meanings to his disciples. People were shocked when Jesus talked about God as if he really knew him. He called God his "Father" and he encouraged his followers to do the same.

The good shepherd stood ready to ward off danger.

"I AM THE GOOD SHEPHERD"

"I am the good shepherd," Jesus told his disciples, in a story he knew they would understand. "A hired man looks after sheep for money, but runs away at the first sign of trouble. The good shepherd cares for his sheep because he loves them. He knows his sheep, and he will give his life to save them."

Seed that fell on shallow soil grew quickly but didn't take root and was soon scorched by the sun.

Seed scattered along the path was eaten by birds.

Seed that landed among thorns was choked.

Seed that fell on good soil produced a healthy crop.

Many people listened to Jesus' sermon from a distance.

Jesus' disciples and close followers sat in a circle around him.

THE SOWER

Jesus began to teach by the lake. "One day a farmer went to sow seed," he said. "Some seed fell on the path, but it was eaten by birds. Some fell on stony soil, but it shriveled up because it had no roots.

Some seed fell upon thorns; it was strangled and died. But other seed fell on fertile soil. It was strong and healthy and grew into a huge harvest." Jesus explained, "This story is about how people respond to God. They are the soil; God's Word is the seed."

THE SERMON ON THE MOUNT

Jesus went into the hills to teach his disciples. A crowd watched from afar. "You will be blessed if you realize your need of God," Jesus taught. "You are like salt sprinkled throughout the world, and like a light

The father was filled with love and compassion when he saw his son.

THE LOST SON

Jesus told a crowd, "A man had two sons. When the younger son asked for his inheritance, his father gave it to him. The young man left home, moved to a foreign country, and wasted all the money on

wild living. When he had nothing left, he took a job looking after pigs because he was so hungry. 'My father's servants live better than this,' he thought. 'I will go back home and say I'm sorry. I will ask my father to give me a job as a servant.'

But when he saw his son, the father ran to greet him, and that night threw a party in his honor. The older son was angry and refused to go. His father explained to him, 'Everything I have is yours. But your brother was lost and now he is found!'"

The shepherd was overjoyed to find the lost sheep.

THE LOST SHEEP

Jesus began, "A shepherd had 100 sheep, but one was missing. He left the other 99 and searched for the lost sheep. When he found it, he was overjoyed." Jesus explained, "In the same way, heaven is happier over one lost sinner who returns to God than over 99 others that were righteous and haven't strayed."

THE LOST COIN

Jesus told a similar story. "Suppose a woman has ten silver coins. She discovers that one is missing, so she lights a lamp and searches the house until she finds it. Then she calls her friends together to celebrate. It is just the same in heaven," Jesus explained. "There is great joy when even one sinner comes back to God."

Jesus told his disciples to love their enemies.

The Samaritan was the only person to help the wounded man.

The thieves ran away after robbing the man.

The priest continued his journey without stopping.

Another religious man, a Levite, crossed onto the other side of the road.

held up for everyone to see. Murder is wrong, but it is just as wrong to hate someone. Love your enemies and pray for them." "How shall we pray?" the disciples asked. Jesus taught them a simple prayer: "Our Father in heaven, hallowed be your name...."

THE GOOD SAMARITAN

One day, a man asked Jesus, "You say I must love my neighbor, but who is my neighbor?" Jesus replied, "A man was traveling along a road when robbers attacked him and left him for dead. First a priest, then a Levite passed by and ignored him. But when a Samaritan saw the injured man, he bandaged his wounds and paid for him to be cared for." Jesus then asked, "Who was the good neighbor?" "The merciful one," the man replied.

The widow dropped her money in the collection box.

The poor guests marveled at the feast.

THE GENEROUS WIDOW

Jesus was with his disciples in the temple. Many wealthy people put money in the collection box, but Jesus noticed a poor widow putting two small copper coins in the box. "That widow has given more than all the others," Jesus said. "The rich people will not miss the money, but she gave everything she has."

THE GRAND BANQUET

Jesus said, "A man invited many guests to a banquet. When the food was ready, his servant went out to call the guests. But they all made excuses to say they could not come. The host was furious, and he sent his servant into the town to invite the poor and the sick instead. 'They are welcome at my table,' he said."

The Death of Jesus

CROWDS FOLLOWED JESUS wherever he went. They came to hear him preach about God and to witness the amazing miracles he performed. But Jesus had enemies too. The scribes, the Pharisees, the Jewish teachers, and religious experts were all jealous of his popularity. When he called God his Father it offended them. When he challenged them to lead good, honest lives, free from hyprocrisy and sin, they were furious. Who was this man, who dared to tell them what God thought! Jesus was a threat to their authority and they waited for an opportunity to get rid of him once and for all.

JESUS ENTERS JERUSALEM
Jesus and his disciples traveled to Jerusalem to celebrate the Passover. The city was teeming with thousands of people who had gathered there for the religious festival. As Jesus rode into Jerusalem on a donkey, crowds threw their coats onto the ground and waved palm branches. "Jesus is King!" they cried.

The meal took place in an upstairs room.

Matthew   Simon   John   Jesus   Peter   James   Judas   James

Thaddeus   Bartholomew   Philip   Andrew   Thomas

THE LAST SUPPER
Jesus and his disciples gathered together to eat the Passover meal. Before eating, Jesus washed the disciples' feet, like a servant. "I am showing you what to do," he said. "You are all equal and you should serve one another." As they were eating, Jesus said, "Someone here will betray me." The disciples were horrified, but Jesus knew that Judas planned to betray him. "I would give up my life for you!" said Peter. Jesus replied, "By tomorrow morning you will deny ever knowing me." Then Jesus took the bread and broke it. "This is my body, given for you. Do this and remember me." Then he took the wine. "This wine is the token of God's new covenant to save you, sealed with my blood."

Jerusalem was crowded with people celebrating the Passover.

Caiaphas, the high priest, accused Jesus of insulting God.

The Jewish leaders could not sentence Jesus to death because Palestine was under Roman rule. They handed him over to the Roman governor, Pontius Pilate.

Jesus had to carry his own cross on the way to the crucifixion site. When he stumbled under the enormous weight, the guards forced a man called Simon of Cyrene to help him.

TRIAL BY THE JEWISH COUNCIL
Jesus stood before the chief priests and the teachers of the law. "Are you God's Savior?" they asked. "Whatever I say you will not believe," Jesus replied. "Are you God's Son?" they asked. "I am," said Jesus. "Enough! We need no more evidence," they said. "To say such things is against God's law!"

TRIAL BY PONTIUS PILATE
The priests took Jesus to Pontius Pilate, the Roman governor. "This man is guilty. He has broken Jewish law," they said. Pilate saw no reason to condemn Jesus, but the crowd outside shouted, "Release the murderer Barabbas! Crucify Jesus!" Pilate did not want any trouble, and so he passed the death sentence.

JESUS CLEARS THE TEMPLE

Jesus went to the temple, which was full of people buying animals to sacrifice to God. In the temple courts, moneychangers had set up their stalls. Jesus knew instantly what was happening and he was furious. These people claimed to be serving God, but really they were making money for themselves! He strode through the temple, overturning the moneychangers' tables. "This is God's house, a place of prayer," he shouted at those selling animals for sacrifice. "You have made it a den for thieves." Once the temple had been cleared, people came to Jesus to be healed. Now the chief priests and Jewish teachers were even more determined to get rid of Jesus.

Peter denied ever knowing Jesus.

BETRAYED BY A KISS

Later that night, Jesus and his disciples went to the Garden of Gethsemane. After a while, a crowd sent by the high priest came to arrest Jesus. They were led by Judas, who had agreed to betray Jesus to the chief priests for 30 silver coins. "The one I kiss will be Jesus," said Judas. The terrified disciples ran away.

PETER'S DENIAL

Jesus was taken to the high priest's house for questioning. Peter secretly followed and waited in the courtyard. "Aren't you one of Jesus' friends?" asked a servant girl. "No," said Peter. Two more people asked him the same question. "No!" he replied each time. As he denied it the third time a cock crowed; it was morning.

Two robbers were also crucified with Jesus. One of them insulted Jesus, but the other one defended him and asked Jesus to remember him. Jesus said to this man, "Today, you will be with me in paradise."

Jesus was put to death on the cross, a Roman method of execution reserved for criminals and foreigners.

A sign at the top of the cross read, "This is the King of the Jews."

When Jesus died, a Roman soldier standing by the cross said, "Surely this was the Son of God."

A group of soldiers threw lots to see who would get Jesus' clothes.

JESUS IS CRUCIFIED

The Roman soldiers led Jesus away. They dressed him in a scarlet robe and placed a crown of thorns on his head. When Jesus reached the crucifixion site, he was nailed to the cross. Mary, Jesus' mother, and a number of his followers watched helplessly as Jesus suffered in agony on the cross. Some people mocked Jesus: "If you are indeed the Son of God, why don't you save yourself?" they sneered. But Jesus said, "Forgive them, Father, for they do not know what they are doing." At noon, the sky turned black and darkness covered the land for three hours. Then Jesus cried out, "Father, I put myself in your hands," and he breathed for the last time.

Jesus Is Alive!

THE DISCIPLES WERE DISTRAUGHT when Jesus was killed. They had lost their leader and they were frightened that the authorities would come looking for them as well. Joseph of Arimathea buried Jesus' body in a rock tomb, and a large stone was rolled across the entrance. But three days later, the tomb was empty. Jesus had risen from the dead! At first the disciples could not believe what had happened, though Jesus had often told them that he would rise from the dead. Before Jesus finally ascended to heaven, he promised his disciples that they would receive the gift of the Holy Spirit.

THE EMPTY TOMB
After the Sabbath, two women went to Jesus' tomb to anoint his body. But when they got there the stone had been rolled away; the tomb was empty and the two soldiers guarding it were lying on the ground as if dead. An angel said to the shocked women, "Do not be afraid. Jesus is risen!"

Thomas touched Jesus' wounds.

The door was bolted.

JESUS APPEARS TO HIS DISCIPLES
The disciples, fearing the Jewish leaders, met together behind locked doors. Suddenly Jesus appeared to them. "Peace be with you," he said. He showed them the scars on his hands, where the nails had been, and the wound in his side. The disciples were overjoyed. Jesus really was alive! But Thomas was not with the disciples, and when he was told what had happened he said, "I will not believe he is alive unless I see the scars myself."

DOUBTING THOMAS
Eight days later, Jesus appeared to the disciples again. This time Thomas was present. "Touch my hands," Jesus said to Thomas. "Stop doubting and believe!" Thomas replied, "My Lord and my God."

JESUS ASCENDS TO HEAVEN
Jesus appeared to the disciples many times after his death. He talked and ate with them, and the disciples had no doubt that he was alive again. One day, Jesus said, "Do not leave Jerusalem until you receive the Holy Spirit, the special gift that God has promised you. When the Holy Spirit comes, you will be able to tell the whole world about me." Shortly afterwards, a cloud shrouded Jesus and he began to disappear up to heaven. As the disciples stared at the sky, two angels appeared next to them. "Why are you looking up there?" the angels asked. "Jesus has returned to heaven, but one day he will come back to earth just as suddenly as he left."

A MIRACLE AT THE BEAUTIFUL GATE
A lame man was begging at the temple when Peter and John went to pray one day. The beggar pleaded with them for money. "I don't have any. But I will give you what I do have." Peter replied. "In the name of Jesus, get up and walk." The man jumped to his feet and followed the disciples to the temple, praising God.

PETER AND JOHN ARE THROWN IN JAIL
People were astonished to see the lame man walking and jumping, but Peter asked them, "Why are you amazed? Faith in Jesus has healed this man." The chief priests were so angry at Peter's preaching that the temple guard flung Peter and John in jail. But thousands of people now believed Peter's message.

The women bowed down before Jesus.

JESUS LIVES!

The two women quickly ran from the tomb to tell the disciples what they had seen. They felt both happy and frightened. Suddenly they saw Jesus; he greeted them and they rushed towards him, kneeling at his feet. "Don't be afraid," Jesus said. "Tell my friends to go to Galilee, where I will meet them."

THE ROAD TO EMMAUS

Later that day, two disciples left Jerusalem for Emmaus. They were talking about Jesus' death when a stranger began to walk alongside them and joined in their conversation. He explained why Jesus had to die. It was only when the disciples reached Emmaus and broke bread with him that they realized he was Jesus.

The disciples struggled with their heavy net.

Peter ran towards Jesus.

BREAKFAST BY LAKE GALILEE

One evening, Peter and some other disciples decided to go fishing. They fished all night, but by morning they still had not caught anything. As they approached the shore, they saw a man on the beach. "Have you caught any fish?" he shouted across the water. "No!" they replied. "Throw your net on the right side of the boat and you will catch some," the man cried. The disciples did as he said, and immediately the net swelled with fish. Peter looked at the stranger. "It's Jesus!" he cried, and leapt into the water. Jesus waited on the beach, warming bread and cooking fish over a small fire. "Bring some of your fish and we can have breakfast together," he said to his disciples.

Many of the crowd accepted Peter's invitation to repent and be baptized.

TONGUES OF FIRE

While the disciples waited in Jerusalem as instructed, they met together in a house for the feast of Pentecost. Suddenly they heard the sound of a strong wind sweeping through the house. Then, small tongues of fire rested on top of their heads, enabling them to speak in many different languages.

PETER ADDRESSES THE CROWD

There was so much noise that a crowd gathered outside the house. Many were foreign visitors who had come to Jerusalem to celebrate Pentecost. They were amazed that the disciples could speak so many languages; they thought they must be drunk! Peter explained that the disciples had received the Holy Spirit.

The two men discussed the book of Isaiah.

THE STONING OF STEPHEN

Stephen was another disciple who had performed amazing miracles in the name of Jesus. When he told the leaders of the Jewish Council that they had disobeyed God and murdered Jesus, they were furious. They dragged him outside and stoned him to death. Saul, who persecuted Christians, looked on.

PHILIP AND THE ETHIOPIAN OFFICIAL

The disciple Philip was traveling on the road from Jerusalem to Gaza when he met an important Ethiopian official sitting in his chariot, reading the Scriptures. "Do you understand what you are reading?" Philip asked. "No," replied the Ethiopian. So Philip told him all about Jesus and baptized him.

The Early Church

THE DISCIPLES WERE NO LONGER fearful and alone. The Holy Spirit had filled them with the power to heal and the confidence to stand up to the Jewish leaders who persecuted them. Thousands of people now believed in their message, and Christianity was born. The new believers changed the way they lived, sharing everything they owned with one another. When they were driven out of Jerusalem, they settled throughout Palestine, taking the message of Jesus with them. Less than thirty years after Jesus' death and resurrection, this message had spread to Rome and beyond.

THE CONVERSION OF SAUL
Saul was on his way to Damascus to arrest followers of Jesus when he was suddenly blinded by a brilliant light. As he fell to the ground, he heard a voice saying, "Saul! Why are you persecuting me?" The terrified Saul asked, "Who are you?" "Jesus," said the voice. In Damascus, Saul was baptized as a believer.

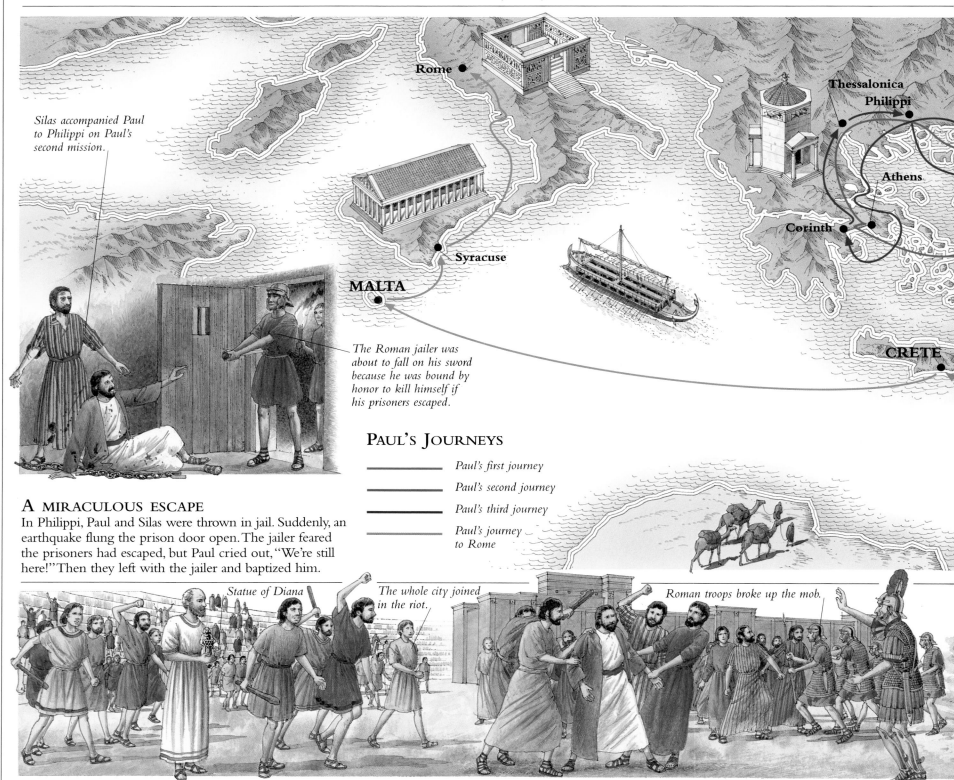

Silas accompanied Paul to Philippi on Paul's second mission.

The Roman jailer was about to fall on his sword because he was bound by honor to kill himself if his prisoners escaped.

Rome

Thessalonica
Philippi

Athens

Corinth

Syracuse

MALTA

CRETE

PAUL'S JOURNEYS

—— Paul's first journey

—— Paul's second journey

—— Paul's third journey

—— Paul's journey to Rome

A MIRACULOUS ESCAPE
In Philippi, Paul and Silas were thrown in jail. Suddenly, an earthquake flung the prison door open. The jailer feared the prisoners had escaped, but Paul cried out, "We're still here!" Then they left with the jailer and baptized him.

Statue of Diana

The whole city joined in the riot.

Roman troops broke up the mob.

THE RIOTS IN EPHESUS
Later, Paul visited Ephesus, where the city's silversmiths earned their living by making statues of the goddess Diana. "Paul is telling everyone that our gods aren't real!" the silversmith Demetrius complained. "If they believe him we'll lose our living." Then they ran through the streets shouting, "Diana is great!"

THE ANGRY MOB IN JERUSALEM
After many years' traveling, Paul returned to Jerusalem. The Jewish leaders had not forgotten him and they stirred up a violent mob, which dragged Paul out of the temple and beat him. News of the uproar reached the Roman commander, who rescued Paul from death, but kept him under arrest.

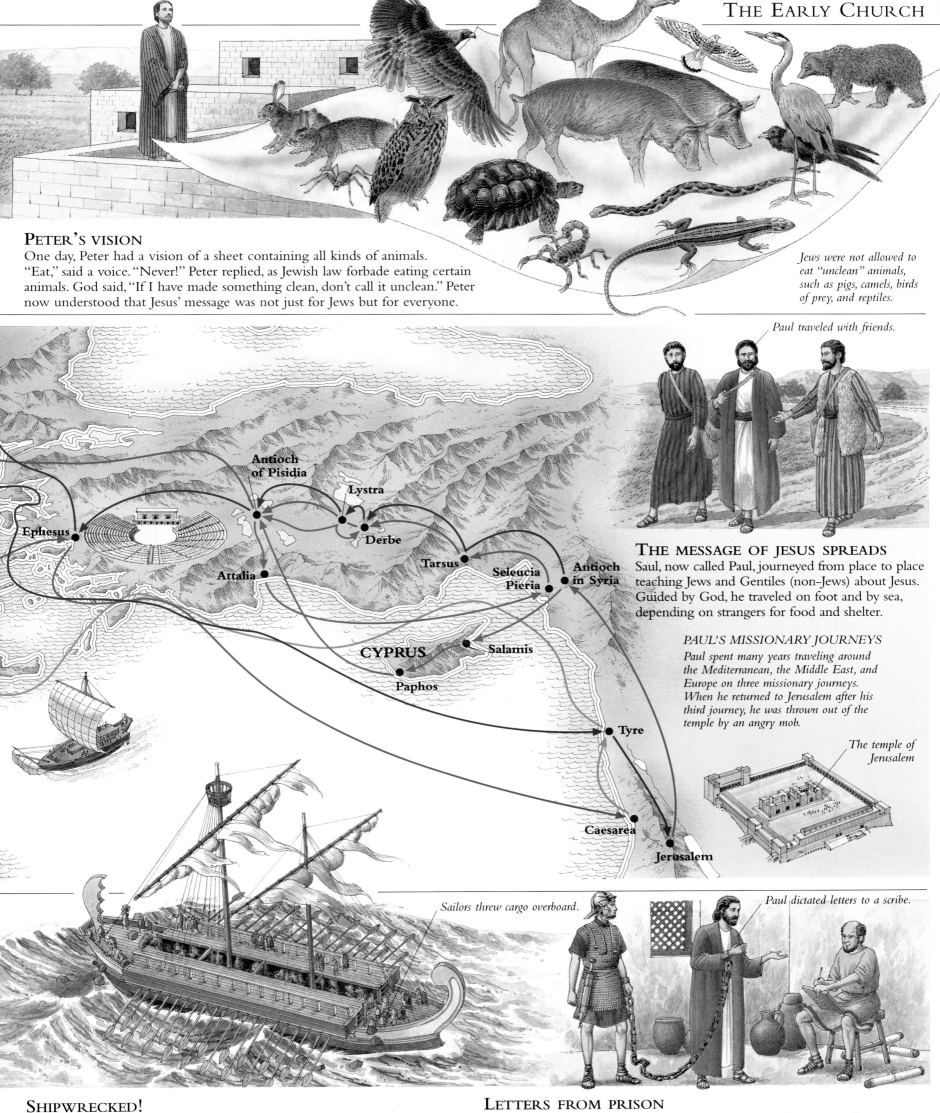

PETER'S VISION

One day, Peter had a vision of a sheet containing all kinds of animals. "Eat," said a voice. "Never!" Peter replied, as Jewish law forbade eating certain animals. God said, "If I have made something clean, don't call it unclean." Peter now understood that Jesus' message was not just for Jews but for everyone.

Jews were not allowed to eat "unclean" animals, such as pigs, camels, birds of prey, and reptiles.

Paul traveled with friends.

Antioch of Pisidia

Lystra

Ephesus

Derbe

Attalia

Tarsus

Seleucia Pieria

Antioch in Syria

CYPRUS

Salamis

Paphos

Tyre

Caesarea

Jerusalem

THE MESSAGE OF JESUS SPREADS

Saul, now called Paul, journeyed from place to place teaching Jews and Gentiles (non-Jews) about Jesus. Guided by God, he traveled on foot and by sea, depending on strangers for food and shelter.

PAUL'S MISSIONARY JOURNEYS

Paul spent many years traveling around the Mediterranean, the Middle East, and Europe on three missionary journeys. When he returned to Jerusalem after his third journey, he was thrown out of the temple by an angry mob.

The temple of Jerusalem

Sailors threw cargo overboard.

Paul dictated letters to a scribe.

SHIPWRECKED!

After two years under house arrest, Paul was taken by ship to Rome to stand trial as a Roman citizen. However, the Mediterranean Sea was treacherous during the winter months, and in a terrible storm the ship ran aground and broke up off the coast of Malta. Paul leapt overboard and swam for the shore.

LETTERS FROM PRISON

Eventually, Paul arrived in Rome. He was kept under house arrest, but was allowed visitors. During this time he sent many letters, teaching and encouraging Christians in the growing number of churches in the Roman Empire. In this way, Paul spent his remaining years spreading the Christian faith.

Index

Biblical references are added in italics so that you can read more about your favorite stories in the Bible.

A

Abednego, 18, 19 *Daniel 1, 3*
Abel, 10 *Genesis 4:1–16*
Abraham, 12–13 *Genesis 11 – 13, 15, 17, 21*
Adam, 8, 9, 10 *Genesis 2 – 3*
Andrew, 21, 22, 26 *Mark 1:16–18, John 6:8*
ark, Noah's, 10–11 *Genesis 5 – 8*
ark of the covenant, 15, 16, 17 *Exodus 25:10–22, Joshua 3*
Artaxerxes, King, 19 *Nehemiah 2*
Assyrians, 18 *2 Kings 18:11*
Augustus, Caesar, 21 *Luke 2:1*

B

Babylon, 18, 19 *1 Chronicles 9:1, Daniel 1 – 6*
Barabbas, 26 *Matthew 27:15–26*
Bartholomew, 26 *Matthew 10:3*
Beersheba, 12 *Genesis 21:33*
Bethlehem, 21 *Luke 2:4*
Bethsaida, 22 *John 12:21*
burning bush, 15 *Exodus 3 – 4*

C

Caiaphas, 26 *Matthew 26:57–67*
Cain, 10 *Genesis 4:1–16*
Caleb, 16 *Numbers 13 – 14*
Cana, 21 *John 2:1–11*
Canaan, 12, 13, 16, 17 *Genesis 12:5–7, Deuteronomy 34:4, Joshua 1:1–4*
Capernaum, 22 *Matthew 4:13*
Cyrus, 18 *Ezra 1:2–4*

D

Damascus, 30 *Acts 9:1*
Daniel, 18, 19 *Daniel 1, 6*
Darius the Mede, 19 *Daniel 6*
David, 16, 17 *1 Samuel 16 – 17, 2 Samuel 2 – 6*
Delilah, 16 *Judges 16*
Demetrius, 30 *Acts 19:24–27*
Dura Plain, 19 *Daniel 3:1*

E

Egypt, 12, 13, 14, 15, 16 *Genesis 37:25, Genesis 46:5–6, Exodus 1 – 11*
Egyptian princess, 15 *Exodus 2*
Elijah, 23 *Mark 9:4*
Elizabeth, 21 *Luke 1:38–56*
Emmaus, 29 *Luke 24:13–35*
Ephesus, 30 *Acts 19:1*
Esau, 12 *Genesis 25:19–34, 27*
Ethiopian official, 29 *Acts 8:26–40*
Euphrates River, 13 *Genesis 2:14*
Eve, 8, 9, 10 *Genesis 2 – 3*
Ezekiel, 18 *Ezekiel 37:4*
Ezra, 19 *Nehemiah 8:1–11*

FG

Feeding the Five Thousand, 22 *John 6:1–13*
Gabriel, 20 *Luke 1:26–38*
Galilee, Sea of, 21, 29 *Mark 1:16*

Garden of Eden, 8, 9 *Genesis 2 – 3*
Garden of Gethsemane, 27 *Mark 14:32–41*
Gaza, 29 *Acts 8:26*
generous widow, 25 *Luke 21:1–4*
golden calf, 15 *Exodus 32*
Goliath, 16 *1 Samuel 17*
Good Samaritan, the story of the, 25 *Luke 10:25–37*
Good Shepherd, the story of the, 25 *John 10:1–21*
Grand Banquet, the story of the, 25 *Matthew 22:1–14*

HI

Haran, 12, 13 *Genesis 11:31*
Holy Spirit, 28, 29 *Acts 1:8, Acts 2:1–13*
Isaac, 12, 13 *Genesis 21, 24, 27*
Israel, 18 *1 Kings 12:21*

JK

Jacob, 12 *Genesis 25:19–34, 27 – 33, 46*
James, 21, 23, 26 *Mark 1:19–20, Mark 9:2–10*
Jeremiah, 18 *Jeremiah 7:3*
Jericho, 17, 23 *Joshua 6*
Jerusalem, 16, 17, 18, 19, 20, 26, 28, 29, 30 *2 Samuel 5:6–10, 2 Kings 25:1, Nehemiah 12:27, Luke 2:41–42, Luke 19:28–44, Luke 23:28, 33, Luke 24:50–53*
Jeshua, 18 *Ezra 3:8–9*
Jochebed, 15 *Exodus 6:20*
John, brother of James, 21, 23, 26, 28 *Mark 1:19–20, Mark 9:2–10, Acts 3:1–10*
John the Baptist, 20 *Mark 1:1–19*
Jordan, River, 16, 20 *Joshua 3 – 4*
Joseph, Jacob's son, 12, 13, 14 *Genesis 37, 39 – 47*
Joseph, Mary's husband, 20, 21 *Luke 1:27*
Joseph of Arimathea, 28 *Matthew 27:57–60*
Joshua, 16, 17 *Numbers 13 – 14, Joshua 1 – 23*
Judah, 18 *1 Kings 12:21*
Judas, 26, 27 *Matthew 10:4, 26:25, Mark 14:43–46*

L

Laban, 12 *Genesis 29 – 31*
Lazarus, 22 *John 11*
Leah, 12 *Genesis 29 – 31, 33*
Lost Coin, the story of the, 25 *Luke 15:8–10*
Lost Sheep, the story of the, 25 *Luke 15:1–7*
Lost Son, the story of the, 24 *Luke 15:11–32*

M

Malta, 31 *Acts 28:1*
Martha, 22 *John 11*
Mary, mother of Jesus, 20, 21, 27 *Luke 1:26–56, John 19:25–27*
Mary, sister of Martha, 22 *John 11*
Matthew, 26 *Matthew 9:9, Matthew 10:2*
Meshach, 18, 19 *Daniel 1, 3*
Mesopotamia, 12, 13 *Acts 7:2*
Michal, 17 *2 Samuel 6:20–23*
Moses, 14–15, 16, 23 *Exodus 2 – 20, Mark 9:4*

N

Nebuchadnezzar, 18, 19 *Daniel 1 – 3*
Nehemiah, 19 *Nehemiah 2:1*
Nile River, 14, 15 *Exodus 1:22*
Noah, 10–11, 12 *Genesis 6 – 9*

OPQ

Passover, 26 *Luke 22:7*
Paul, 30–31 *Acts 9:1–31, 13 – 28*
Pentecost, 29 *Acts 2:1*
Peter, 21, 23, 26, 27, 28, 29, 31 *Mark 1:16–18, Mark 9:2–10, John 13:37, John 18:25–27, John 21:1–10, Acts 2, Acts 3:1–10*
Pharaoh, 13, 14, 15 *Genesis 40 – 41*
Philip, 26, 29 *Matthew 10:3, Acts 8:26–40*
Philippi, 30 *Acts 16:12*
Philistines, 16 *Judges 16:30*
Pontius Pilate, 26 *Matthew 27:11–26*
Promised Land, 16 *Joshua 1*

R

Rachel, 12 *Genesis 29:6–30*
Rahab, 17 *Joshua 2, Joshua 6:15–25*
Rebekah, 12, 13 *Genesis 24, 27*
Red Sea, 15 *Exodus 13:17–22, 14*
Rome, 30, 31 *Acts 28:11–16*

S

Samaria, 22 *John 4:4*
Samson, 16 *Judges 13 – 16*
Samuel, 17 *1 Samuel 1 – 3, 8*
Sarah, 12, 13 *Genesis 21*
Satan, 9, 20 *Genesis 3, Matthew 4:1–11*
Saul, King, 17 *1 Samuel 9 – 11, 13 – 19*
Saul (the apostle), 29, 30 *Acts 7:55 – 8:1, Acts 9:3–6*
Sermon on the Mount, 24 *Matthew 5 – 7*
Shadrach, 18, 19 *Daniel 1, 3*
Sheba, Queen of, 17 *1 Kings 10*
Shiloh, 17 *1 Samuel 1:24*
Silas, 30 *Acts 15:22 – 19:10*
Simon, the disciple, 26 *Matthew 10:4*
Simon of Cyrene, 26 *Matthew 27:32*
Solomon, 16, 17, 18 *1 Kings 2 – 3, 5 – 8*
Sower, the story of the, 24 *Matthew 13:1–23*
Stephen, 29 *Acts 6:8 – 7:60*
Susa, 19 *Nehemiah 1:1*

T

tabernacle, 15 *Exodus 26 – 27*
temple, Solomon's, 16 *1 Kings 5 – 8*
Ten Commandments, 14, 15 *Exodus 20*
Thaddeus, 26 *Matthew 10:3*
Thomas, 26, 28 *Matthew 10:3, John 20:24–31*
Tigris River, 13 *Genesis 2:14*
Tower of Babel, 11 *Genesis 11:1–9*
Transfiguration, 23 *Mark 9:2–10*

UVW

Ur, 12 *Genesis 11:31*
wise men, 21 *Matthew 2:1–12*
woman at the well, 22 *John 4:7–14*

XYZ

Zacchaeus, 23 *Luke 19:1–10*
Zedekiah, 18 *Jeremiah 52:1–11*
Zerubbabel, 18 *Ezra 3:8*